How many Nursery Rhymes do you know?

How many questions can you answer?
It's fun to peek behind
the flap — to see if you
were right …

PRICE/STERN/SLOAN
Publishers, Inc., Los Angeles

Hickory, dickory, dock, what ran up the clock?

Who went to the cupboard to fetch her poor dog a bone?

What was in the dainty dish set before a king?

Who sat on a wall, and had a great fall?

Rub-a-dub-dub, how many men in a tub?

What frightened Little Miss Muffet away?

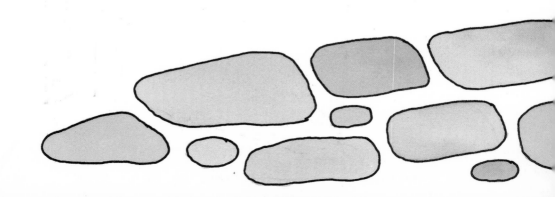

Who was a merry old soul?

It's raining, it's pouring, who is snoring?

Hey diddle, diddle, what jumped over the moon?

Who lived
in a shoe?

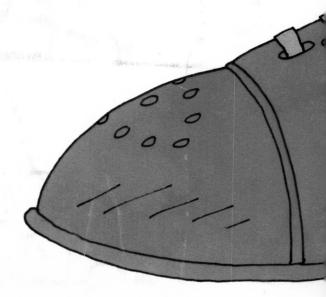